Call Me Mattaniah
A Shepherd Meets Jesus

Written by Martha Graham
Illustrated by Barbara Dye

While Mattaniah is a fictional character, the accounts of all events are Biblical.

Victoria Fletcher
Hoot Books Publishing
851 French Moore Blvd.
Suite 136 Box 14
Abingdon, VA 24210

Chapter 1
Matty and the Lamb

My name is Mattaniah. To some of you, I probably seem like an old man. Actually, I am now 43 years old. I'm a Jewish shepherd in a large field about seven miles outside Bethlehem. I was born a shepherd, born into a whole family of shepherds. In fact, my ancestors as far back as the time of our Father Abraham were shepherds.

My friends used to call me Matty when I was younger. Mattaniah is an old family name. It was a hard name for my friends to say, but something happened when I was a young boy that caused me to want to be known by my real name, Mattaniah. I'll tell you about that in a few minutes.

But let me start my story from many years ago – 1400 years ago, in fact. My father and my grandfather have told me this old story so many times that I know it by heart.

All those years ago God chose my ancestors, Abraham, Isaac, Jacob (also known as Israel), and their descendants, to be His people. At the time when they had become slaves in Egypt, God instructed Moses to lead His chosen people – the Israelites, who were also known as

Jews – out of Egypt to Canaan, which God promised them as their forever home. Now this wasn't just a few people. No! There were at least 2,000,000 people – that's 2 million men, women, and children! More than 13 times the number of people who cram inside the Bristol Motor Speedway for a race! And besides all those people, they took with them lots of animals!

It would be a long journey to Canaan. Because the people sinned early in the journey, they had to wander in the desert for 40 years before they reached Canaan.

During all those years, however, God was faithful to the people He had chosen as his own. He stayed with His people. He cared for them and led them. And He gave them a visible sign that He would always be with them wherever He led them.

He told Moses to build a Tabernacle, or *Mishkan* in the Hebrew language, which means "dwelling place." It would be made up of a tent and a fenced outside courtyard.

The tent was about twice as long as a modern family room, perhaps in your house (45 feet to be 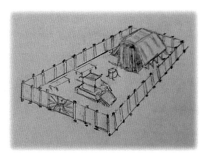 exact). It could be disassembled so the people could carry it with them wherever God led them.

 Inside the tent were two rooms, the Holy Place and the Holy of Holies. A beautiful, embroidered curtain separated the Holy Place from the Holy of Holies. God Himself told Moses that He would dwell – or *tabernacle* with them – in the Holy of Holies room of the Tabernacle! Because God dwelt there, the Holy of Holies was a very, very special place. There was only one piece of furniture inside, known as the Ark of the Covenant. The Ark was a large gold-covered box, with three items inside: a jar of the 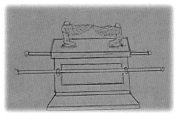 manna that God had provided as food for the Israelites on their journey; the shepherd's rod that had belonged to the High Priest Aaron,

which God had miraculously caused to bud and produce almonds; and a copy of the Ten Commandments that God had given to Moses. On its top, the Ark was covered with a gold-covered lid, called the Mercy Seat. On top of the Mercy Seat stood two gold cherubim whose wings touched each other. God dwelled in this room, in this Holy of Holies, between the cherubim.

There was a fenced courtyard on the outside of the tent where a large water basin, called a *laver*, and an altar were set. As you already know, from the time of the very first people God created, Adam and Eve, every single person sinned. So every single day, two lambs had to be sacrificed on the altar, one in the morning and one in the evening, in order to cover the sins of the people. God required that these lambs be very special lambs – they had to be one-year-old and PERFECT – no spots or blemishes. Every day. Day after day. Twice a day. Two perfect lambs every day.

In keeping with God's very specific instructions, once a year the High Priest would cleanse his hands and feet outdoors in the laver; then he would sacrifice a bull on the altar in the courtyard for his own sin, along with a lamb and other animals for the sins of the people. Finally he took some blood from the sacrificed animals, through the beautiful heavily embroidered curtain, into the Holy of Holies and sprinkled it on and around the Mercy Seat. When God saw the sprinkled blood of the sacrifices, He covered the people of their sins for another year. That was called *Atonement*. And this was done every single year for the 40 years that the people wandered in the desert and for more than 400 years when they lived in Canaan.

After they had been in Canaan many years, King David, Israel's greatest king ever,

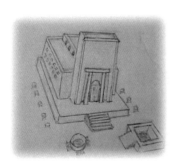

desired to build a permanent dwelling place, or Temple, for God in Jerusalem. David gathered all of the materials, and his son, Solomon, built a Temple where God would dwell. Solomon put the Holy Place and the Holy of Holies of the Tabernacle inside this magnificent Temple. Inside the Temple, a single, heavy, beautifully decorated curtain again separated the Holy Place from the Holy of Holies. All of the sacrifices still took place at the Temple altar just as they had at the Tabernacle altar, including two perfect lambs every day and a bull and a lamb once a year. That beautiful Temple remained in Jerusalem for 450 years, even after Israel itself divided into a Northern Kingdom (called Israel) and a Southern Kingdom (called Judah).

In spite of God's faithfulness to these people whom He had chosen, they sinned so badly that they again had to bear the consequences. The Northern Kingdom was overcome and taken captive by the Assyrians. Later, the Babylonian King Nebuchadnezzar captured Judah and took the people to Babylon and destroyed the Jerusalem Temple. This happened more than 500 years before Jesus was born. All of the people mourned, of course, because they loved their Temple and because that's where they had worshiped God. It just wasn't the same for them!

After the people spent 70 years in exile in

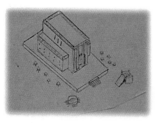

Babylon, God kept His promise and allowed them to return home. They rebuilt the Temple in Jerusalem where the people could offer sacrifices and worship God. It was not nearly as beautiful as the original Temple that Solomon had built. But for another 500 years, people came to the Temple day after day, offering perfect lamb after perfect lamb, along with other animals that God required, to cover their sin temporarily.

When my grandfather was a young shepherd boy, King Herod expanded the Temple. It is still a magnificent Temple where we worship God and offer sacrifices to the God who has been faithful to his people, Israel, all these hundreds of years.

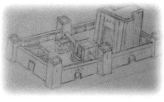

Now this is where I come in. As a young shepherd, I – Matty – I saw the most incredible sight in all the world!

Remember I told you that our family had raised sheep for thousands of years? Well, these aren't just any sheep; they are the perfect, spotless lambs that God required to be sacrificed at the Temple. When I was 10 years old, my father allowed me to care for the most precious lamb on my own. He was perfect! He was spotless! Of course, I knew that he eventually would be chosen to be sacrificed but while I cared for him, I loved him with all my heart.

One night as we shepherds were tending our flocks, we saw something so spectacular that I could hardly believe my eyes! All at once, the heavens opened up and this angel appeared and spoke to us and told us not to be afraid. The angel told us that a Baby had been born that very day in the city of David (Bethlehem), and that this Baby was the Savior, the Messiah, Christ the Lord! The angel said we would find this Baby wrapped in swaddling clothes and lying in a manger – a manger! A dirty stone feeding trough just like my lamb ate from! How could this be? Well, we were just beginning to clear our eyes when a whole host of angels appeared praising God and saying, "Glory to God in the Highest, and on earth peace, goodwill toward men!"

We were so frightened and excited at the same time!

And just like that, the angels were gone!

So what did we do? We ran as fast as we could the seven miles to Bethlehem. We were so excited that those miles felt as though we had taken a single step!

All of a sudden, we came to a stable outside an inn, and there we found Him. He reminded me of my little lamb, but oh, so much better! Beautiful! Perfect! Spotless! I had never before seen anything so wonderful in all my young life. I just knew that this was the Messiah, the Lamb of God, that all my family, for all my life, had been talking about and waiting for. I fell on my knees right in front of that dirty old stone feeding trough, which his father had lined so tenderly with hay, and I worshiped that little Baby, Jesus Christ our Lord!

After a while, we had to leave and get back to our own sheep. I knew, though, that my life would never be the same after that. I finally understood all of those lambs that had been sacrificed for hundreds and hundreds of years. I knew that this Baby I saw was the Lamb of God and that He would give His life so that everyone who ever lived could be saved from their sins. I knew that the animals' blood that had been sprinkled year after year in the Holy of Holies would no longer have to be spilled. Somehow Jesus' blood would cover all sins for all time for all people who believe in Him. I didn't fully understand, but I did know that God had sent a wonderful gift to the world!

Oh, yes, one other thing changed for me that night. No longer did I want to be called Matty. Now, I wanted everyone to call me by my real name – Mattaniah – which means *Gift of God.* God had sent His true Gift <u>to me</u> and <u>to everyone</u> on earth, and He had allowed me to see His Gift with my very own eyes. I would be honored to bear the name my parents gave me for all my life.

Chapter 2
Mattaniah and the Lamb of God

Remember me? I'm Mattaniah. We met in the last chapter. I told you how my father and my ancestors before him had been shepherds in Israel. For hundreds and hundreds of years, my family has tended the flocks of sheep offered as sacrifices at both the Tabernacle and later at the Temple in Jerusalem.

Do you remember that I told you that every lamb that was sacrificed had to be perfect? Twice a day, every day, two perfect lambs, were sacrificed for the sins of the people.

We also talked about the most sacred room in both the Tabernacle and the Temple, called the Holy of Holies. This was where God dwelled among His people. Once each year, the High Priest would cleanse himself, then go through the side of the beautiful, heavy, embroidered, one-piece curtain into the Holy of Holies and sprinkle the blood of the sacrificed animals on the Mercy Seat of the Ark of the Covenant. When God looked on the blood on the Mercy Seat, He covered the people of their sins for another year. It was a solemn day but it was also a day of great rejoicing when the High Priest came out of the Holy of the Holies for the people knew God had covered their sins.

Every day as I have tended the flocks of sheep for the Temple, I have remembered the night when I was ten years old when the skies opened and the angels appeared, announcing Good News for all people and praising God. I've remembered going to Bethlehem and finding the Baby lying in a manger, just as the angel said we would. As I looked into the sweet and gentle eyes of the Baby that night, I fell down beside that dirty old stone manger, and I worshiped Him. I still remember looking at the Baby that night and thinking He was even more precious than my own first little lamb. I've thought of Him so many times through the years – when I was a teenager and when I married my wife and as our children grew up. I've told them all about the precious Baby I saw that night.

I've thought even more about Him lately. A couple of years ago, I heard that John had baptized a Man and declared Him to be "the Lamb of God who takes away the sins of the world." And then, they say, heaven opened, and God called this Man his Son! My heart quickened when I heard that, and I again remembered that special night I heard the angels declaring Good News and praising God.

I have continued to hear stories about this Man whose name is Jesus, which means "God saves." He calls Himself *the Good Shepherd*. They say He has healed people and performed all kinds of miracles. So I started to think: Could this Man, this Jesus, really be the Baby I saw that night?

For the past week, the city of Jerusalem has been very busy since it is Passover season. All Jewish men have come to Jerusalem for the feast to celebrate God's leading our people out of Egypt. There are so many people! Everywhere! Crowds and crowds of people!

.

And then, just last Sunday, in these crowds, I saw Him! I had come to Jerusalem to deliver sheep to the Temple. As I walked around the city afterward, I found myself at the foot of the Mount of

Olives. And there I saw Him. I saw the Man riding on a donkey while people scattered palm branches before Him and praised Him. He rode right past me! I looked into His eyes and I knew I had seen those eyes before! The Baby! He was the same Jesus! Such a perfectly gentle and humble Man he was.

On Friday – the day we Jews prepare for the Sabbath – I was still in Jerusalem. I heard that three men were being crucified that very day. What an awful death those Romans used on the vilest criminals! I thought the men must have done something horrible to be sentenced to death that way. I'd never seen a crucifixion, and frankly, I didn't want to see these crucifixions either.

As I made my way into the city later that same day, I saw Jesus again! But now I could hardly recognize Him. He had been beaten to the point that He looked nothing like He had on Sunday when I had seen Him on the donkey. But again I looked into His gentle eyes, and I knew it was Him. And then I realized that the sweet, perfect Baby I had worshiped by the manger more than 30 years ago was one of the three men being crucified. The difference in the three men was that this One, Jesus, was not guilty of any sin or crime! Instead,

He was dying for the sins of the world.

I thought my heart would break within me! I couldn't help it. I followed Him. I sat beneath His cross all day, even as the sky grew pitch black for three hours in the middle of the day. I saw the sign they put above His head, "This is Jesus, the King of the Jews." I heard the people yelling insult after insult at Him. I heard the two criminals arguing even as they hung dying on crosses next to Jesus. I heard one of those criminals place his faith in Jesus as the Savior and King. I heard Jesus assure that criminal that he would be with Jesus in paradise. I heard Jesus ask His Father to forgive the ones who crucified Him. I heard Jesus cry out to His Father with a loud voice, "It is finished!" I watched Him die. And at that very moment, the earth shook, rocks split, and tombs broke open. Even the soldiers were terrified and acknowledged that this Jesus was the Son of God.

I heard lots of excited shouts about the Temple veil – that beautiful, heavy, embroidered, one-piece curtain in front of the Holy of Holies. People were saying that it had split in two from top to bottom!

Even in all of the commotion, I stayed beneath His cross. I watched Joseph of Arimathea and Nicodemus take Jesus' body down from the cross to bury Him. I had never been so sad in my whole life.

I sat weeping for a long time before I could stand to go back to the field. Sabbath would begin soon, lasting from sundown on Friday until sundown on Saturday. I had to get home before it began for I wouldn't be allowed to travel that far once the sun had set. My legs would hardly carry me as I trudged the seven miles back home. The question *Why did He have to die?* rang through my mind over and over and over. I hardly slept at all that night. The next day, the Sabbath, everyone seemed even more subdued than usual. That night, again, I hardly slept. I just kept seeing His beautiful, loving eyes.

When I went back into Jerusalem on Sunday morning, there was an unusual clamor throughout the streets of the city, and everyone was talking about an unbelievable event. I tried to listen in on people's conversations wherever I could.

Many were talking about this Man Jesus who had been crucified on Friday. They said His tomb was empty and that He was no longer dead but had been raised from the dead!  Could it be? Was that even possible?

Then I remembered the words of the angel that night more than 30 years ago, "...for unto you is born this day in the city of David, a Savior, who is Christ the Lord." Of course! This Baby – this Jesus – was indeed the Messiah, Christ the Lord, the Lamb of God who takes away the sins of the world. Just as the old prophets had foretold hundreds of years before, He had died for me and been raised back to life to take away the sins of everyone on earth who had faith in Him. And now He would live forever in heaven and would invite all who repent of their sin and believe in Him to live eternally with Him.

And no more animals would ever again have to be sacrificed! I was happy for all of my lambs, but I was especially happy that my sins and all of the sins of all the people of the world could now be forgiven because Jesus, the Sweet Lamb of God, had been sacrificed for all who would believe in Him and invite Him into their hearts.

The joy I felt was so great that I had to run home and tell my family everything I had heard and seen. I even told them about that heavy one-piece curtain in front of the Holy of Holies being torn straight down the middle, from top to bottom, to show people that they no longer needed the High Priest to intercede with God for them. Now they - Jews and all other people - could talk directly to God for forgiveness of their sins.

Of course, because I was a shepherd, I had to go back into Jerusalem regularly to deliver sheep. One day as I walked, I thought I spotted Jesus again. I doubted my eyes, but then I heard others saying they, too, had seen the Man who had died, been buried, and was now alive. When I caught up with Him again, I could see it really was Jesus. I saw the nail scars in His hands and feet, and I saw His eyes, looking straight at me as He asked me, "Do you believe in Me?" Right there on that busy, dusty street, I fell at His feet and worshiped Him as my Savior, Christ the Lord. I'll never forget that moment!

A few weeks later, I overheard men talking about Jesus again, but this time they were telling how Jesus had been taken up into heaven right before their eyes and then a cloud hid Him from their sight!

Angels had appeared again. They reassured the men that their Friend, this same Jesus, would come back. The men, whom Jesus had called His apostles, suddenly remembered that Jesus had told them that He could come back and take them to heaven and not just them but all who would put their faith in Him. My heart almost beat out of my chest! Jesus coming back for me? To take me to heaven to live forever with Him? How He must love this shepherd boy! And how deeply I loved Him!

19

As I have reflected on all these things, my name becomes more meaningful to me every day. Mattaniah. Gift of God. My parents gave me that name because they believed that I was a gift given to them by God.

But now I know that God has given all of us His most precious Gift: His Son. And I will praise Him forever for giving us His Lamb!

Romans 10:9-10

"If you confess with your mouth the Lord Jesus and believe in your heart that God has raised Him from the dead, you will be saved. For with the heart one believes unto righteousness, and with the mouth confession is made unto salvation."

Your Bible contains much more information about the accounts in our story.

CHAPTER 1

The Sacrifices. Numbers 28

The Tabernacle. Exodus 25:8
"And let them make Me a sanctuary,
that I may dwell among them."

God gives Moses the plans for the Tabernacle. Exodus 25:1-31:11

The Israelites build the Tabernacle. Exodus 35-Exodus 40

  Court.
      Walls. Exodus 38:9-20
      Basin/Laver. Exodus 38:8
      Altar. Exodus 38:1-7
  Tent.
      Holy Place. Exodus 37:10-29
      Holy of Holies (Most Holy Place).
          Veil (Curtain).Exodus 36:35-38
          Ark of the Covenant. Exodus 37:1-5
          (Aaron's rod. Numbers 16-17)
          Mercy Seat. Exodus 37:6-9

God's glory fills the Tabernacle. Exodus 40:34-35

The Temple.2 Samuel 7:13

"He (Solomon) shall build a house for My name, and I will establish the throne of his kingdom forever."

David gives Solomon the plans God had given to him.1 Chronicles 28:11-12

King Solomon builds the Temple.1 Kings 5:1-8:11, 2 Chronicles 2:1-5:14

God's Glory fills the Temple.2 Chronicles 7:1-3

The Temple destroyed by King Nebuchadnezzar. Jeremiah 52:12-13

The Temple rebuilt by Zerubbabel. Haggai 1-2

The Temple expanded by King Herod. Not detailed in Scripture; see http://jewishencyclopedia.com/articles/14304-temple-of-herod

The birth of Jesus in Bethlehem. Luke 2:1-7

The angels appear to shepherds in fields near Bethlehem. Luke 2:8-20

CHAPTER 2

The birth of Jesus in Bethlehem. Luke 2:1-7

The angels appear to shepherds in fields near Bethlehem. Luke 2:8-20

John baptizes Jesus. Matthew 3:13-17; Mark 1:9; Luke 3:21

God declares Jesus His Son. Matthew 3:16; Mark 1:10-11; Luke 3:22-23

Jesus heals many people. Matthew 4:24; Luke 4:40; Luke 5:15

Jesus performs many miracles. Mark 6:2; Luke 19:37; Acts 2:22

Jesus' entry into Jerusalem. Matthew 21:8-11; John 12:12-15

Jesus' crucifixion. Matthew 27:32-56; Mark 15:22-37; Luke 23:32-46; John 19:17-30

Joseph of Arimathea and Nicodemus bury Jesus' body. John 19:38-42

The empty tomb. Matthew 28:1-16; Mark 16:1-8; Luke 24:1-12; John 20:1-18; 1 Corinthians 15:4

The curtain (veil) of the Temple torn in two. Matthew 27:51; Mark 15:38; Luke 23:45

How Jesus, the Sweet Lamb of God, atoned for the sins of the world. John 3:16; John 1:29

Jesus ascends into heaven. Acts 1:1-11

About the Author and Illustrator

Martha Graham, the author, is a retired education administrator with a love for Scripture and making it accessible to people of all ages. Her goal for this book is that all readers will see the God of the Bible through the eyes of a child who loved his lamb and a man who came to truly know, accept, and love the Lamb of God.

Barbara Dye, the illustrator, is a retired nurse. Her lifelong artistic interests have been displayed in drawing and painting such varied subjects as cartoon figures on the sides of her barn to reverent scenes on church baptistries. Her thorough research of the details is evident in the line drawings of this book. Barbara's greatest joy is to see people come to know the Lord.